ELMER'S EGG

**Story and pictures
by Bernard Wiseman**

SCHOLASTIC BOOK SERVICES
NEW YORK · TORONTO · LONDON · AUCKLAND · SYDNEY · TOKYO

For Pete, Mike, and Andy.

ISBN 0-590-32762-3

12 11 10 9 8 7 6 5 4 3 2 1

Printed in the U. S. A.

3 4 5 6/8

09

One day Elmer the Elk

saw a bird in a tree.

The bird was sitting

on something

round and white.

"What are you sitting on?"
asked Elmer.

"It is an egg," said the bird.

Suddenly the egg began to crack,

and out came a baby bird.

"Ah," Elmer said.

"I've always wanted

a baby brother.

Now I know how to get one."

"First I have to find an egg,"

said Elmer.

Elmer looked and looked.

He saw something on the ground.

It was round.

It was white.

"This must be an egg,"

Elmer thought.

"I will sit on it

and a baby brother

will come out."

Elmer sat

and sat and sat.

Then Elmer looked.

He did not see

a baby brother.

"COME OUT!" Elmer yelled.

The bird flew over.

"Did you call me?" it asked.

Elmer said, "No.

I was yelling at my egg.

I sat on it,

but nothing came out."

The bird said,

"You must make a NEST.

That is where to sit on eggs."

Elmer asked,

"How do you make one?"

The bird showed Elmer

how to make a nest.

Elmer put his egg

in the nest.

Elmer sat on his egg again.

He sat

and sat and sat.

Then he looked.

He still did not see

a little brother.

"COME OUT!" Elmer yelled.

The bird flew over again.

"Did you call me?" it asked.

Elmer said, "No.

I was yelling at my egg.

I put it in my nest,

I sat on it,

but nothing came out!"

The bird looked at the egg

and said,

"That is not an EGG at all.

That is a STONE.

You must sit on a REAL EGG.

Then something will come out."

Elmer climbed down the tree.

18

Elmer found

an old football.

He found

an old baseball,

a balloon,

a pumpkin,

and a watermelon.

Elmer asked the bird,

"Is one of these an egg?"

The bird said, "No.

None of those are eggs."

Elmer cried,

"Please give me an egg!

I want to make

a baby brother."

The bird said,

"My eggs make BIRDS.

You need an ELK egg."

Elmer asked,

"Where can I get

an elk egg?"

The bird said,

"You must LAY one."

Elmer asked,

"How do you lay an egg?"

The bird said,

"Sit in your nest,

say TWEET, TWEET, TWEET,

and an egg will come out."

Elmer sat in his nest.

He said, "TWEET, TWEET, TWEET."

Then he looked.

He did not see an egg.

"COME OUT!" Elmer yelled.

The bird flew over again.

"Did you call me?" it asked.

"No," said Elmer.

"I was talking to my egg.

I sat in my nest,

I said TWEET, TWEET, TWEET,

but it didn't come out."

The bird said,

"Go see the CHICKENS.

They lay lots of eggs.

Maybe they can tell you

how to do it."

Elmer ran to the chickens.

He said, "Chickens,

tell me how to lay an egg."

A hen said,

"I flap my wings.

I say CLUCK, CLUCK, CLUCK.

That is how I lay an egg."

Elmer did not have wings.

He flapped his front legs

and said,

"CLUCK, CLUCK, CLUCK."

Just then a rooster said,

"COCK-A-DOODLE-DOO!"

Elmer asked,

"Should I say that too?"

The hen said, "No.

ROOSTERS say that.

Roosters can't lay eggs.

Roosters are BOYS."

Elmer cried,

"I am a boy too!"

The hen said,

"Then you cannot lay an egg."

Elmer cried,

"I HAVE to lay an egg!

I want to make a brother."

The hen said, "A BROTHER

cannot make a BROTHER!

He would be

his BROTHER'S MOTHER!

And a BROTHER

cannot be a MOTHER!"

The rooster cried, "Yes!

Only a MOTHER

can be a MOTHER!

Only a MOTHER

can make a BROTHER!"

Elmer ran home to his mother.

"MOTHER!" he yelled.

"Make me a BROTHER!"

Elmer's mother said,

"I was going to tell you.

I am making one now."

Elmer looked around.

"Where is the NEST?"

he asked.

"Where is the ELK EGG?"

His mother said,

"There is no nest.

There is no egg to see.

I am making your brother

INSIDE ME!"

Elmer yelled, "COME OUT!"

His father came out

of the house.

"Did you call me?" he asked.

Elmer said, "No, Dad.

I was calling

my little brother.

I want him to come out!"

Elmer's father said,

"He cannot come out yet.

He is still too small.

You must wait awhile."

Elmer waited

and waited

and waited.

Then one day

Elmer's mother said,

"Here is your little brother.

His name is Edwin Elk."

Elmer yelled, "COME OUT!"

Elmer's father asked,

"Why did you yell

COME OUT?

Your brother is here!"

Elmer said,

"I know Edwin is here.

I yelled COME OUT

because I want Edwin

to COME OUT AND PLAY!"